Girl in a

By

Claire Boley

Independently published

Copyright Claire Boley 2024

The right of Claire Boley to be identified as

the author of this work has been asserted in accordance with the sections 77 and 78 of the copyright.

Design and Patents Act 1988

All rights reserved

No reproductions, copy or transmission of this publication may be made without written permission.

No paragraph of this publication may be reproduced, copied or transmitted without the written permission of the author or in accordance with the provision of the Copyright Act 1956 (as amended)

This book is a work of fiction.

Names, characters, places and incidents originate from the writer's imagination any resemblance to actual persons, living or dead is purely coincidental.

First independently published in 2024

Also by

Claire Boley

If Only I'd Listened

False Teeth

Girl in a Bedsit

By

Claire Boley

Chapter 1

I soon arrived at Covent Garden Tube Station from Knightsbridge, before I knew it I was putting the key in the door of my bedsitter in the building across the road from the Theatre Royal, Drury Lane. Peace reigned thank God, while I made a cup of tea and watched the six o'clock news. It must have been eight o'clock when my door bell rang. As no one ever visits me without an invitation, I sat wondering who the hell it could be when who ever it was started banging as loud as possible on the door. The banging made me anxious that I decided to ring into my neighbour Wendy, to get her to look through her spy hole on to the landing.

*****

Earlier in the day I'd been over to the Rendezvous Restaurant in Basil Street, Knightsbridge. I love it in this particular restaurant and often visit for the mushroom omelette and chips. I usually need to queue for at least half an hour before my order is taken, as the restaurant's very popular – I believe it's worth the wait especially for the omelette. Today I was lucky as there were only a few people in the queue, this must have been because the sun was shining and the locals had wandered over to Hyde Park. I suppose I could have bought sandwiches and gone there as well. The thing is I have a problem with Hyde Park and sandwiches, back along I sat down on the grass and before I realised my sandwiches were being eaten out of my hand by the pigeons.

Once I ordered my meal I sat myself down at the end of a bench next to a complete stranger who didn't say a word until my food arrived then out of the blue he chatted non stop about my omelette and how he wished it was his. The waiter explained that it was mine and if he wanted something to eat he needed to join the queue to put in an order. "I thought it was waiter service. Surely you can take my order."

"I don't take orders. I bring your food to the table once it has been ordered and cooked. You need to join the queue." replied the waiter nodding his head towards the queue. "If I do what you have said I may lose this seat as I doubt if this young lady will save it for me. Please take my order."

"I've already told you once that I don't take orders, you need to join the queue. If this young lady won't agree to save your seat, you'll have to chance your luck about finding another table to sit at once you have put your order in. What I am suggesting is what everyone does." This conversation continued while I sat looking down at my food as if I wasn't interested in what they were saying even though I could hear every word. I had the shock of my life when I eventually decided to turn and take a closer look at this chap with the BBC accent, he looked as if he hadn't a bean to his name – even his shoes were falling apart. Where he lives I dread to think. Mind you there are a lot of people out there like him, he's not the first I have met and I doubt if he will be the last and some live in posh apartments. "I'll keep this seat for you but once I've eaten my meal I'll be on my way."

"I better get a move on."

"You had." With that he immediately jumped over the bench and hurried along to the end of the queue which was now out the door due to it being lunch time. After a while he returned smiling to himself as if he was the cat that had got the cream. "Thank you for saving the seat."

"While you were in the queue two people asked to sit down but I managed to persuade them to go else where."

"Thank you. It's a wonder you saved the seat for me the way I look."

"I never go by looks. You talk with the BBC accent which is good enough for me." The man burst out laughing.

"What's so funny that you have to laugh at me?" Leaning over he explained that he had just come out of prison after a stretch of two years. Being told this I was in a state of shock and didn't know what to do or say.

"Don't look so worried I'm harmless enough. I only stole money from people I worked with. I've never burgled a house or anything like that."

"Why did you get two years? That's a hell of a stretch, you must have done something terrible. I reckon you took a gun out and pretended to shoot the person you were stealing from."

"That's for me to know and you to find out." He blushed.

"It could have been a knife that you threatened someone with. I'm good at guessing and I'm usually right. I can tell by your face that it was one or the other."

"I'm out now and I intend to go straight."

"Until the next time."

"It is bloody awful inside. I can assure you there won't be a next time. I didn't even have a cell to myself. The bloke I shared with was a homo, he kept trying to touch me up and telling me how good sex was with a man, he reckoned it was far better than with any woman."

"Shut up you shouldn't be telling me that."

"Sorry getting back to you, where do you hang out and what do you do for a living?"

"I've got more sense than to tell you anything." With that his meal arrived so silence reigned.

"If you haven't any manners, I'm going to move to a different table or leave the restaurant altogether, as your manners are appalling – I'll vomit in a minute, you make me feel sick."

"Sorry, I am forgetting where I am. I thought I was still inside."

"Well, you're not, you're sharing a bench with me in the Rendezvous Restaurant in Basil Street, Knightsbridge."

"Who's me? What's your name?" I thought for a minute and decided not to tell him my real name and definitely not where I live. "I'm Marjorie from around the corner." I replied lying through my teeth.

"You're telling me that you live around the corner from here?"

"That's what I said."

"You must have plenty of dosh or a bloody good job, as it must cost an arm and a leg to live here."

"It does but it's well worth it, for the type of person I can associate with."

"Out of interest which street do you live in? It was more luck than judgment that I came across this place so I'd never find your particular street. I'm staying in a hostel for ex-prisoners up by St Georges Hospital. I asked the bloke on the door which way I should go as I needed to get some food in my belly. This is what he suggested, 'If you're feeling rich turn left when you get out on the pavement, keep going and you'll bump into Knightsbridge, you'll soon find somewhere to eat, whether you can afford the food is another matter. If you feel poor go straight across the road from here to Hyde park then walk across to Oxford Street, you'll soon come across a cheap and cheerful café.' I decided to turn left and finished up here, not that I'm rich and can afford this type of food every day." I changed the subject back to his name. "I've told you my name so you may as well tell me yours." Like me he took ages to reply. "I was baptised Thomas. Most people call me Tom."

"Right Tom, tell me which prison you were in?"

"Wormwood Scrubs in Du Cane Road."

"I know it. I wouldn't enjoy sleeping there for one night let alone two years. Hardened prisoners are put in the scrubs so you must have done something very bad to get a bed in there."

"I told you what I did, I stole a few pounds out of my mates coat pockets while they were working." He laughed then continued "I always made sure I left enough money in the coat pocket for the person to get home by tube or bus."

"That was generous of you." I said sarcastically.

"One day I decided to pinch the money from the shop till and I got caught red handed. The police arrived and took me to the station, the rest is history."

"Tom I would never dream of doing anything like that. I'd rather be poor than steal someone else's hard earned cash and get caught into the bargain. I have never heard of anyone being put in the Scrubs for just stealing a few pounds. I have a feeling you got a gun out when you got caught." Tom looked stupid.

"Yes I did, I didn't fire it, in fact it wasn't even loaded."

"Where were you working?" Tom stared at me for a few minutes before replying. "Woolworths, New Oxford Street. I was the under manager until I went in the nick." he blushed.

"All I can say is that you were stupid, as Woolworths is quite a good place to work especially if one is working from the office, like you must have been. I know people who would have given their right arm to work there. What are you going to do for a job now you are out of the Scrubs? As I know damn well Woolworths won't take you back, it's no good thinking they will."

"I'm not sure but I know I have to find some where to live before applying for any job, as firms won't take anyone on unless they have an address."

"You have a big problem on your hands. I hope you have the money in your pocket for a deposit on a bed sitter?"

"I have enough money for that, at least I think I have. The governor gave me a few pounds when I left the Scrubs. Me coming here today and having this meal is a big treat. I won't be coming again in a hurry."

"Tom, I hate the thought of you or anyone for that matter having to sleep under Waterloo Bridge with the down and outs due to lack of money but I can see it happening to you if you don't sort yourself out."

"I slept there for a couple of nights before I went in the nick."

"So have I slept there but I wouldn't like to think I had to go back to sleeping there again." I said making a face.

"The biggest problem I found with sleeping under the bridge was the lavatory, it's quite a distance from where one sleeps and some of the down and outs pee where they lay."

"God almighty, I didn't see any of that the couple of nights I slept there. Whatever else are you going to tell me?"

"Move closer so I can whisper in your ear." Like a fool I moved along the bench.

"Hurry up Tom, I need to leave once you've told me more of your rubbish."

"Sometimes the down and outs crouch down next to the wall and perform – it's not a pretty site and the smell is horrendous."

"I don't want to hear any more." With that I immediately got up and rushed out the door, ran along to Hans Crescent then to Harrods and across the road to the tube station, where I hurried down the escalator to the Piccadilly line. Once on the platform, I had the shock of my life, walking towards me was Tom. He must have followed me out of the restaurant then decided to come down on to the platform from the Sloane Street end. Whether he saw me remains to be seen as he didn't show any sign of recognition. I only had to wait a few minutes before the tube arrived, luckily the carriage door opened directly in front of me. I jumped on board and found a seat near the entrance. Once I settled myself down all I could do was pray that Tom would be getting off the tube at Hyde Park Corner – that's if he got on board. The tube soon arrived at Hyde Park Corner where I sat and watched the passengers including Tom walk along the platform. I guessed he was making his way back to the hostel and out of my life for ever. Little did I realise he jumped back on the tube further along the platform.

****

Chapter 2

The phone rang and rang, there was no reply, most probably Wendy had already gone to her favourite watering hole – The Wellington, she goes there most evenings and definitely on a Saturday. I cannot imagine who's knocking my door as I haven't many friends but the ones I have wouldn't dream of standing outside on the landing banging the door like a madman. After the person had spent a good five minutes knocking I decided to shout as loud as I dare at the door. "What's up, who are you, why are you banging on my door?"

"It's John the door man, I am trying to wake you. I thought you must be a sleep as you haven't answered the bell Miss Hilary." With that I opened the door.

"What the hell do you want? You're frightening me to death with all your banging."

"There's a chap downstairs who has asked me if he can come up to see you as he wants to have a chat, the thing is Miss Hilary he looks a bit shifty. I questioned him knowing you but he insists he met you at the Rendezvous, where ever that is."

"John, how he found out that I live in this building I don't know. All I can think is that he must have followed me from the tube station. Another thing, I didn't tell him my real name. Don't let him come up here, please send him packing" I must have sounded annoyed as John started to shout at me.

"Keep your hair on girl. I'll go and send him back to where I think he came from, which I guess must be Waterloo Bridge."

"Thanks john, I feel such a fool as I never dreamt for one minute that he would follow me home then have the nerve to ask if he could come up here. It's a darn good job we have a doorman like you, who is the receptionist come telephone operator. If we didn't have you I guess this Tom would have knocked on every door until I answered. I definitely didn't tell him my real name or where I lived, so how the hell he did know where to come to find me and who to ask for? I have a feeling he must have seen me get on the tube at Knightsbridge then at the next stop which was Hyde Park he took a chance by getting off the tube and getting back on again in the carriage behind the one I was in then when he saw me get off at Covent Garden Tube Station he jumped off to follow me. John this is the scary bit why did he feel the need to follow me of all people? What odds is it to him where I was going or where I live, he's a stranger to me."

"He asked me for Miss Hilary."

"Please go and get rid of him. Remember what I'm about to tell you. If he says his name's Tom, he's been in the Scrubs for two years and only came out the other week – he stole money from where he worked and got caught red handed."

"I'm going. I hope he isn't downstairs trying to open the safe to get the petty cash tin."

"John, hang on a minute, I walked from the tube with a friend perhaps he heard my friend say 'goodbye Hilary'. In a few minutes I'm going over to the Wellington, please make sure you get rid of him – straight away."

"I promise I will." With that John got in the lift to go down to the ground floor. I went back in my room to glam myself up.

Once down stairs I opened the main door out on to Drury lane and cautiously looked out, luckily for me this so called Tom was nowhere to be seen. I rushed across the road to Broad Court which is the cut through to Bow

Street and the Wellington Public House, this only took a few minutes. Along the way I glanced towards the phone kiosks in Broad Court and noticed that one kiosk had cardboard packaging up the inside as if someone is sleeping there. I immediately thought of Tom and wondered if he is sleeping just across the road from where I live?.

Once in the Wellington it took me a while to find Wendy and her mates as they were sat right at the back. Wendy was in shock to see me as I very rarely join her in any pub unless it's a high day or holiday.

"God almighty, look what the wind's blown in, Hilary from next door. Why the hell have you come to join us? You don't even drink alcohol regularly, something serious must have happened for you to put your feet in here." called out Wendy.

"I've had a terrible day. I need some booze to get me over it." I sat myself down on the one and only empty stool and explained what had happened and how this man had followed me home. Wendy and her mates appeared shocked and decided to buy me a drink.

"What would you like, a lager or something stronger?" asked one of the men who jumped to his feet.

"Something stronger than lager, I'd love a Gin and Tonic please."

"Gin it will be, by the way I'm Tim." He said holding out his hand for me to shake. He soon returned from the bar carrying a tray of drinks. I took my glass and before I knew it I'd drunk it down and was waiting for a second. If my parents had been here they would have been frog marching me out of the pub, as I don't know when to stop drinking once I start and often finish up on the floor. Back along I made a fool of myself at a wedding by passing out after too much alcohol.

"Sorry Hilary the next round is on me and I'm not getting you another Gin as I don't want to carry you home." laughed Wendy. "I can remember you at that wedding the other week. It's a coffee for you." I sat with my head between my hands feeling like a naughty school girl. The evening progressed with me getting quieter and quieter and Wendy and her mates getting louder. By ten thirty they were all in some state and began to sing – show me the way to go home. After a few minutes the bar maid came over and suggested that we should all leave and showed us to the side entrance.

"Which way are we walking?" asked Wendy looking a bit squiffy.

"You know damn well which way we go Wendy after an evening in the pub and that is along to Trafalgar for a paddle in the fountains." Replied Tim looking annoyed.

I never dreamt for one minute that Wendy of all people would be going in the fountains with her mates but she did. If I'd had more Gins I'd have joined in the fun then regretted it for the rest of my days. I was in shock when they all striped to there underwear, leaving their outer clothes in a pile alongside Nelson's Column.

"Come on Hilary get your clothes off." Shouted Tim, while clapping his hands to encourage the others to join in and they did. "Don't be a bore Hilary." They all shouted then one bright spark started to shout and clap on his own. "Strip, strip I dare you to strip."

"I'm not into this sort of thing."

"Hilary, you may as well go home if you're not going to join in the fun as you come over as a complete and utter bore." Shouted Wendy. I felt such a fool that I immediately took off my shoes and ran over to the nearest fountain with all my clothes on, God it was cold, the others followed in their underwear. We all stayed in for a good fifteen minutes splashing each other. Once out I stood shivering and wished I had taken my clothes off so I had dry ones to put back on, I wondered how we'd dry ourselves and get warm. Tim's mate who seemed to be more of a bore than me got a couple of bath towels out of his ruck sack and offered them around – ladies first. Once we were sort of dry Tim offered us all a swig of Brandy, apparently Wendy and her mates jumped into the fountains most Saturday evenings and one of them always brought the brandy – this week it was Tim's turn. Wendy took the first swig then passed the bottle over to me. I didn't know whether to take a swig or pass the bottle on as I didn't think mixing a Gin with a swig of Brandy was a good idea, as I've known people to become hooked on this concoction.

"Not for me thanks." Wendy looked peeved.

"Why the hell did you come across to the Wellington knowing full well that you were only going to have the one alcoholic drink all evening then to crown it all refuse a swig of Brandy? We're all hardened drinkers, aren't we boys and girls?"

"Yeah, we are." They shouted in harmony.

"I didn't intend coming to the Wellington for just the one drink I intended having a few and you Wendy wouldn't get me a second Gin due to how I behaved at the wedding the other week. If I'd known you were coming here after an evening in the pub I'd have left after the first Gin especially after you refused to get me a second. You listen to me Wendy dear, I've known people to mix a Gin with a Brandy and have it as their favourite tipple then before they knew what they were doing they were alcoholics and guess what, within six months they were digging up the daisies."

"Hilary, I remember the wedding over in Fulham Palace Road as if it was yesterday, I will never forget it. You got pissed out of your mind then fell over on the floor, it took a few of us to get you back up on your feet. I'm not going to say what happened next as it was too embarrassing for words. You getting pissed at the wedding is the reason why I wouldn't buy you another Gin. You could have gone up to the bar and got your own."

"Stop arguing the pair of you. A single Brandy on top of one Gin won't kill you, it will help you to get home." Laughed Tim.

"Alright, give it here, I'll take a swig then I'm going." All five of them stood around to see what happened to me which was nothing – thank God. "Hilary, you look as if the end of your world has arrived and why are you looking down at your dress?" asked Tim.

"Because my dress is wet and I have to walk home looking like a drowned rat."

"Don't look so worried Hilary." Called out Tim while looking in his ruck sack for another dry towel. "here you are," he shouted throwing a towel towards me. "Make sure you bring your own next week." Once I'd dried myself I handed the towel back to Tim. "Hilary, keep it, give it back to me next Saturday."

"I doubt if I will be here next Saturday as I'd far rather have a cup of tea or a mug of coffee than a glass of alcohol. Mind you I have enjoyed your company and I love it in the Wellington – that was my first visit."

"That's good, we'll see you next Saturday, around eight." Called out Tim ignoring what I said about preferring a cup of tea or a mug of coffee.

"If I turn up and it is a very big if, perhaps you could introduce yourselves to me properly as I only know you and Wendy by name."

Chapter 3

I left Wendy and her mates standing under Nelson's column watching me walk across Trafalgar Square to St. Martin's Lane. It wasn't long before I was walking down Long Acre towards Drury Lane and home. The only people I bumped into along the way were rough sleepers that were getting organised to spend the night in a door way opposite Covent Garden Tube Station. One of the girls stood in my way and asked where I was going as I looked a bit of a mess and wondered if I needed somewhere to sleep. My answer to sleeping was no but I did stay for a chat.

"How long have you been sleeping on the streets?" I asked. "About a month. Mum kicked me out, as she was fed up with the type of person I was mixing with." Said the youngest of the two girls near to tears. "One evening and after a few drinks I invited these friends home to meet mum – once they had left mum went ballistic and suggested I should leave home the following morning. Morning came and like a fool I pretended nothing was wrong – my first mistake. ' This is the last meal you're having here my girl so make the most of it.' I was in shock. I honestly didn't think she

would say 'get out' once she'd slept on it but she did. She gave me half an hour to pack my bags once I'd finished eating my breakfast."

"Did she give you any money?"

"Yeah a five pound note, enough to catch the tube into the West End and have a few pence left over." Nodding towards the men I asked how long they'd been sleeping rough. "Years apparently. I met them over at Charing Cross Station a couple of weeks ago and have been living with them ever since." answered the same girl.

"Before I ask any more questions or answer any of yours, please tell me your names so I know who I am talking too. I'm Hilary from Salisbury."

"I'm Mary-Ann from Hampstead, North London." Said the girl who was kicked out from home.

"John is my name but close friends call me Jo – I'm Jo to you." Said the man who was making the coffee. "That's Pete over there." Said jo nodding his head towards the other man.

"I'm Annie." Said the second girl holding out her right hand to shake mine. "I've been sleeping rough for a number of years. I left my foster home in Yorkshire years ago and haven't heard or seen my foster family since I walked out the door, my foster mum could be digging up the daisies for all I know. I will always remember how good she was to me. I didn't get on with my foster dad – he was very strict and often gave me a slap."

"How long did you live with them?"

"Years, my foster mum told me that I moved from my birth parents place when I was six years old. I was lucky as I stayed with the same foster parents until I was sixteen, not like lots of children who move from one foster home to another."

"Another question for you Annie, why were you put into care?"

"I have no idea, I asked my foster mum that once but she wouldn't tell me, she said social services didn't say. Whether that was true or not I don't know, sometimes I think it's better not to know the answer to that, at least I don't have to worry about the reason."

"Where the hell do you sleep when it rains?"

"it has only rained the once since I've been sleeping rough and that was in the night – thank God. That particular night I was lucky enough to get on the late night bus but I had a problem, I only had enough money for a ticket to the first stop. After paying the conductor I rushed upstairs, made myself comfortable and fell asleep. When I woke I found myself in the Old Kent Road bus depot, just when the bus drivers were coming on duty for the morning shift. I managed to get my things together and jump off before they saw me." replied Mary-Ann.

"Gosh, that was a bit of luck, they could have got you to pay for your night's kip." We all laughed.

"It wouldn't have been with money, as I hadn't a bob to my name once I'd paid my one stop fare. I'm not stupid I know damn well what they would have wanted so they didn't report me. Enough of that, they didn't catch me so they didn't have to ask and I didn't have to give, thank goodness. Getting back to you Hilary, where are you going?"

"Home to my room, across the road from the Theatre Royal. I enjoy living there but like most people I have a few hang ups, the main one being my room which is on the fifth floor. I always go to bed worrying about what could happen if there was a fire in the building as the lift wouldn't be working. I don't fancy having to climb out the window on to a fire man's ladder or even worse having to be carried down to the ground floor as I am not very good with heights. I've been living in this small dingy room for a couple of years, before living here I was like you lot living on the streets. I was lucky enough to be given a tent by a woman I got chatting with at Paddington Station and it was big enough for me and all my bits and pieces, I would have hated being like you four using sleeping bags on the open ground."

"How the hell did you get back to having a roof over your head? Being given a tent by some kind soul isn't the same as having a room."

"I was very lucky. I met a chap called Graham in the coffee bar behind the National Portrait Gallery. Graham worked in the city but slept rough."

"How did he manage to have a job without having a room? I thought you had to get a room before you can get a job."

"You lot ask a hell of a lot of questions."

"We all need to know the answer to this one, then perhaps we can get a room somewhere." Annie laughed.

"Graham pretended to be living in a flat over in the East End with his Gran. This make believe Gran let him visit her once a week for a bath, she also let him use her address for his mail which he picked up when he visited."

"Why the hell didn't he move in with this woman?"

"Because she only had the one bedroom, also she was far too old for Graham to be interested. He was only in his early thirties and this old woman was a pensioner and had to be at least sixty plus."

"I understand now, it would have been like living back at home with his mum but without a bedroom."

"How did Graham meet her?" called out Pete.

"He bumped into her one evening on the way to where he was going to sleep – where ever that was. She had dropped her basket of shopping all over the pavement. Graham stopped to help pick it up, afterwards they stayed chatting and she suggested that he used her place for a bath once a week and her address for his post."

"That was a bit of luck on his part. How did you get involved with him?"

"Quite easily, most evenings I went to the coffee bar behind the National Portrait Gallery, Graham was like me sat on his own, we got chatting across the tables. In a strange way I found him quite interesting so I arranged to meet up with him every evening for a week or so then out of the blue he invited me to move in with him. I was in shock 'what do you mean by moving in?' I asked 'I'm happy enough living in my tent which is big enough for me and all my bits and pieces.' He was taken aback to my reply as he seemed to think he had fallen in love with me and he thought I felt the same way, which of course wasn't true."

"What the hell happened next, Hilary?"

"I stayed away from Trafalgar and the coffee bar for a good month. I managed to find somewhere else to go for my coffee, in fact I moved into this area and had a coffee in that bar." I said pointing towards it. "One evening when I was bored stupid I wandered back to Trafalgar to see if Graham was still around. I looked in the coffee bar window and sure enough there he was, sat at the same table on his own doing the Times crossword just like he did a month ago. I knocked on the window, Graham looked shocked but pleased at seeing me looking in at him that he immediately ran out to greet me. We were both so happy to see each other that we decided to meet up as we did before by having a coffee every evening. It took him six months to pluck up the courage to ask me to move in with him for a second time. I doubt if you will believe this but he had managed to save up most of his spare cash just in case he bumped into me again. Now you know how I managed to get a room. The sad thing about all of this is that Graham moved out after a couple of weeks as we were as different as chalk and cheese and found we couldn't live together full time. I shall always be grateful to him for getting me off the streets and into a room as it helped me to get a job."

"Where do you work?"

"In the accounts department of Harrods – I'm good with numbers."

"Would you like a coffee?" shouted Jo who was sat a distance from us. "Yes please, I need something to warm me up, my mates and I went for a paddle in a fountain over at Trafalgar – the water was freezing even though it's the Summer."

"I thought your dress looked a bit on the damn side."

"And everything else I have on. The thing is I went in fully clothed as I was too embarrassed to undress." The coffee didn't taste bad considering it was made using stale coffee powder and the thermos was filled with hot water first thing in the morning and now it's getting on for midnight.

"Before I go, I have a question. How long have you lot been bedding down here?"

"Only a couple of weeks, it's not a bad spot except when the wind blows up the hill from over there." replied Jo pointing across the road. "In the evenings we go around the back of that café and take the stale food out of the skip, some of it is only a couple of days out of date and still tastes yummy."

"I am wondering why you and Pete live on the streets?"

The two men looked at each other, Jo who was the chatter box explained how they had arrived in London together from Hertfordshire five years ago. They were so fed up with village life that they decided to move to the city and have lived on the streets ever since.

"Where do you come from Hilary?" asked the bloke called Pete.

"Salisbury. I don't go home very often, my parents ask too many questions about my life. I hate questions. I don't think it is any of their business how I live."

"My dad is always trying to get me to go back home." said Pete. "I'm not for going home – I love London. Even if I live like this for the rest of my days, I'd rather be in London town."

"I'm pleased I met Graham even though we only lived together for a couple of weeks, at least I got a room out of him. I was very fortunate as he managed to save enough money for the deposit on my bed sitter." I laughed. "What's this room of yours like?" asked Mary - Ann.

"Very small and needs a good coat of paint. It consists of a single bed, a small cupboard and a wash basin. I can sit on the edge of my bed and have a lick and a promise. The bathroom and lavatory are down the corridor."

"That sounds far better than what we have. We go down that hill to the public conveniences for a wash and brush up. Some conveniences are better than others, the Covent Garden ones are not bad which is another reason for us staying around this area."

"I'm going on my way, thanks for the coffee, try and get a good night's sleep." I started to walk across the road when I decided to ask another question. "Have any of you ever bumped into a chap that calls himself Tom with a BBC accent? I have a funny feeling that he's living rough near the Wellington."

"I know him." Answered Peter putting his hand in the air. "He used to sleep here but I managed to get him to move on. Whatever you do Hilary don't get friendly with him as he'll pinch your last penny,"

"I have a feeling he sleeping in one of the phone kiosks in Broad Court." I went on to explain what had happened and Mary – Ann suggested I avoided him and Broad Court area like the plague. "Thanks for your advice. I shall take it on board, as I definitely don't want him trying to befriend me. I hope I never bump into him again."

Chapter 4

Once in bed I laid awake for ages worrying about Wendy, had she returned home and was already asleep or was she still in the fountains with her mates? The thing is I've never heard her return from any of her boozy nights so perhaps she goes home with a mate and returns to her room in the morning.

What I'm going to do today I don't know as it's Sunday and I can't go to a pub like most Londoners as the smell of the alcohol tempts me to drink more than I should.

Thank God last evening Wendy's friends listened to her when she told them not to get me a second alcoholic drink. Wendy knew about my drinking habit as she was with me when I fell over at the wedding and cut my forehead open then had to go by ambulance to the Casualty Department at St. Thomas's Hospital to have a few stitches. I felt such a fool as the Casualty Sister insisted that I stayed in overnight to sober up. The staff nurse who was on duty the following morning suggested that I should go along to Alcoholics Anonymous with her the following Saturday. I never dreamt in my wildest dreams that this staff nurse had a drink problem, I thought perhaps she was going along to help out at the meeting but no she was an alcoholic. The following Saturday morning Barbara the staff nurse and I met up at Leicester Square Tube Station then walked along to the hall where the A.A. meeting was being held. I was in shock when Barbara explained that she had been coming here at least once a week for a good year. "I never dreamt nurses drank alcohol as if it was going out of fashion."

"Most do. I was caught red handed one lunch time by my Ward Sister in the staff cloakroom having a quick swig from a bottle of Sherry."

"Barbara, I can't stand Sherry and getting caught drinking it from a bottle by my boss would have been the last straw for me. It wouldn't have been so bad if I'd been caught drinking something I like. My favourite tipple is either Vodka or a Gin and Tonic."

"The thing is Hilary, I have never enjoyed dishing out the meals for the patients – it bores me silly. This particular lunch time I decided to go to the staff cloakroom with my friend the bottle. I was in terrible trouble when I got caught and was told to join Alcoholics Anonymous immediately. If I hadn't agreed I would never have worked as a nurse again – I would have lost my pin number. Now I have told you about me and my friend you can tell me about you and yours."

I thought for a minute and came up with this wonderful story which was a complete and utter lie but sounded good. It was about my parents being alcoholics and how from the age of ten they kept giving me a drop of what they were drinking.

"God almighty Hilary, it's a wonder you didn't finish up in care."

"Well I didn't, thank God. I've finished up living on my own in one of the smallest bedsitters in Covent Garden. My life is very lonely, my only real friend is the bottle."

"I suggest you try to give up the booze or you may finish up like me coming here at least once a week for the rest of your days. Mind you Hilary we could always meet up and come along together."

By now we were walking through the front door into the hall where quite a few people were sat around waiting for something to happen. If I didn't know any better I would have thought they were waiting for a séance to take place. After a while a very prime slim lady arrived introducing herself as Angela and explained that she's the chair person who will be taking the closed meeting this morning. After saying the A.A. prayer we all took it in turns to stand and introduce ourselves then explain how we managed to avoid having any booze to drink this week. Some said they went for a walk around the streets, while others mentioned doing extra house work. One of the men caught the train over to Reading to visit his mum, while there he cut the lawn and did odd jobs around the house. A couple of the women had not managed to go without alcohol for the week. Angela asked them both in turn how much they had drunk, they looked at each other as if they were not going to answer, then out of the blue Anne who looked the elder of the two decided to talk nonstop about her week.

"On Monday I was so fed up with my life that I drove to my local super market bought as much booze as I could afford which included six bottles of red wine along with a bottle of Whisky."

"Then what happened Anne?"

"I went home and started drinking. The next thing I remember it was Wednesday afternoon and I was sat on my bedroom floor in a pool of urine." Everyone looked embarrassed for her.

"Anne, how much do you think you drank altogether?" asked Angela.

"I have no idea. When I came to my senses, I went downstairs where I found six empty bottles of wine on the kitchen worktop. Thank God I hadn't drunk any of the Whisky."

"Have you anything to say about your week Christine?"

"Only that I went to the White Horse pub behind Selfridges. I arrived there at about twelve noon Wednesday and stayed until I was kicked out."

"What did you drink?"

"I remember starting with a pint of Guinness and finishing with a short. I have no idea what I drank in between. I put the key in the door to my flat in the early hours of Thursday morning."

"You won't be seeing me here again." I called out.

"Why ever not, Hilary.?" Asked Angela. "You won't get off the alcohol unless you have help from us here at A.A."

"I will, you just watch me. I'm not like any of you." I replied, with that an elderly lady from the group came over for a chat. "Look at me." Said the lady standing up proudly.

"What about you?"

"I've been coming here for over twenty years and I still call myself an alcoholic, even though I don't drink a drop of alcohol. I can't walk into a pub as I know I wouldn't be able to stop myself from asking for an alcoholic drink. One drink would lead to two, and so on and so forth, eventually I'd finish up on the floor."

"What is or was your favourite tipple?" I asked.

"It used to be farm house cider – scrumpy, if I could get it. If I went into a pub today I'd drink anything as long as it was cheap and cheerful." Angela looked across and nodded as if to say it was my turn to introduce myself. I repeated the story that I told Barbara. I'm not sure if any of the alcoholics believed me, in fact I know damn well they didn't because of the way they looked at me, their look said 'liar'.

After me it was Barbara's turn, she rambled on explaining how she had worked extra shifts in the Casualty Department at St.Thomas's Hospital due to shortness of staff. Once she got home from one of her shifts she immediately opened a bottle of her favourite tipple and drank the lot "I couldn't resist opening and drinking the strongest red wine I had in the cupboard – I was exhausted and desperate for a drink." Looking embarrassed Barbara turned and walked away from the meeting and sat in the far corner of the room to have a good cry. I went over to console her. "I feel such a fool. I wish with all my heart that I could give up my friend. The problem is that most of the hospital staff drink and encourage each other to drink more than they should. The difference between me and the rest of the staff is that they have never been caught taking a quick swig on duty then being sent to one of these meetings."

"Barbara, I have a suggestion to make, empty your place of all the booze you have – pour it down the sink then get rid of all the empty bottles including the glasses so you are not reminded of alcohol."

"That sounds a brilliant idea, whether I can do it or not is another matter."

"I'm willing to come around to your place – where ever that is, to give you a hand. I got rid of all my drink and glasses like that. It doesn't mean I don't dream about having a drop because I do, but I haven't a glass to drink it out of. Drinking alcohol straight from a bottle is not very lady like. Barbara if you don't want to throw the drink away you can always give it to a friend who enjoys a drop of the hard stuff and has no intension of giving it up."

"When I'm having a swig I forget about being a lady, the booze takes over. Back along I took myself out to lunch and ordered a meal plus a bottle of red wine which I drank before I finished the meal. I remember talking to a couple at the next table, they got fed up with me rambling on that they left without finishing their meal or saying goodbye."

"Barbara, you sound a bit like me on a bad day. Here's a tissue, dry your eyes, then perhaps we can leave before getting collared by Angela and have to stay till the end of the meeting. Pick up all your bits and pieces and hurry out the door with me, to find a coffee bar where we can sit and have a chat."

"Hilary, I know a place just around the corner from here, I often visit especially after coming here. It's tiny but very cosy and the coffee is yummy and well worth the money."

Eventually we arrived in the coffee bar and settled ourselves down at a table right at the back where Barbara started chatting nonstop about her life and how she married a young doctor in her early twenties but divorced him within a year -it finished because he was alcohol mad and encouraged Barbara to drink far more than she should every time they went out together. "My parents realised why I fell for Steve, he was charming – he even managed to charm mum until she saw how much he drank and how he encouraged me to do the same. He never once asked for a cup of tea when visiting my parents. His favourite tipple was Campari – not a gentleman's drink you are going to say but Steve loved it."

"I quite enjoy a Campari, especially with lemonade but I wouldn't drink more than two or three in one sitting. Barara, tell me more about your ex and what made you marry him knowing he drank far to much for his own good?"

"I used to bump into Steve at the hospital, he worked on the same ward as me as a houseman. I fancied him rotten, when he asked me out for a drink I jumped at the idea. I couldn't wait for him to get me into bed but he never invited me. One evening I took the matter into my own hands and suggested having sex. His answer was no as he didn't want to make love to me unless we were married, like an idiot I agreed to marry him. I thought he loved me but I soon found out he loved alcohol far more than he would ever love me. I'm changing the subject over to my friends dinner party, what happened made me smile and may do the same for you. This lady had taken along a bottle of wine. The wine she took they didn't drink during the meal so when they went into the sitting room for coffee the lady asked where her wine was even though she had helped consume two bottles of strong red wine during the meal. My friend's boyfriend went and fetched the wine plus a glass and poured the lady a drop, by the time she went home she had drunk the lot. I can't imagine how she felt the following morning. I guess she must have had a thick head – serves her right I say." We both had a giggle.

"Is your friend still a friend of this lady?" I asked.

"No, she has not seen or heard from her since. Getting back to my ex-husband and his drinking, my parents were very upset with his behaviour as they could see me having to give up my nursing career just because of him and his best friend. My parent know nothing about me having to come to A.A. If I told them I have a feeling they would disown me. I'm pleased that we have met and both feel the same way about giving up the alcohol. Tell me about you and your friend the bottle."

"My heavy drinking days started just after I left home, they got a lot worse once I started sleeping rough. I doubt if you will believe this but rough sleepers always seem to find money for alcohol, where they find it I don't know. The ones I got friendly with managed to get hold of Gin, so Gin is what we drank." I went on to explain how I met Graham. "Hilary, that was a bit of luck you bumping into him, your life must have changed for the better overnight."

"I guess it did but I couldn't give up the booze which made Graham so cross that he walked out after a couple of weeks but often called in to see how I was getting along and sometimes stayed for a few nights – when he felt rich he gave me a few bob."

"He sounds like a good friend, with benefits."

"I haven't seen him for over a year, I reckon he's found someone else more suited to his life style. If my parents knew what I'm about to tell you they would be so disgusted I think they would kill me or like yours disown me."

"I'm all ears." replied Barbara, looking around to make sure no one was listening in.

"You must remember this happened long before I met Graham and before I got the job in Harrods. I gave oral sex for either booze or a couple of pounds to buy the booze. I didn't mind who I went with as long as I had the booze. The rich men gave me Gin the poor gave me Cider, unless they ran off without giving me either."

"Oh my God, I wouldn't have done that for anything, think of all the infections you may have picked up in your mouth then down through your oesophagus to your stomach and intestines."

"Trust a nurse to think of that. From what you are saying it seems I was very lucky, any way infections were the last thing on my mind, booze was far more important than any bug." Silence reigned for a few minutes then out of the blue Barbara changed the subject and started talking nonstop about the evening she went out with her mates for a boozy time and how she tripped over her feet while wearing stiletto heels finishing up in casualty with a broken ankle.

"God, it hurt and all they would give me for the pain was Paracetamol."

"Why didn't you ask for a couple of Codeine Phosphate? Being a nurse I thought you would have asked for something like that when they offered Paracetamol."

"This happened long before I started training. I had just finished my A levels at tech. I fell over while out celebrating my results."

"Come on Barbara, tell me why you couldn't take something stronger than Paracetamol? There must have been a darn good reason for not. You have me wondering now."

"I was about sixteen when a doctor gave me two Codeine Phosphate tablets for pain relief. Hilary, please don't ask what happened to me to need these tablets because I honestly can't remember. Anyway after taking a few I started hallucinating. My parents were in a terrible state as I saw all sorts and they could not see any of what I could see. If it had been Christmas we wouldn't have needed to put up decorations specially for me as I could see them in every room in the house including the loo, all in different shapes, sizes and colours. One night when going to sleep, as well as seeing decorations a large pot full of plants came flying towards me. Once I stopped taking the pain killers the hallucinations eased off a bit and stopped completely after three weeks. Thank God."

"That must have been scary."

"It was. I'm never taking them again, in fact it's in my notes at the Doctors Surgery saying not to give them to me. I wouldn't recommend them to anyone – not even my worst enemy."

Chapter 5

We carried on chatting when out of the blue Barbara asked me if I had any ambitions. "Not really. I'm happy doing the accounts in Harrods. Have you?"

"Yeah I would love to open a nursing home, it has been my dream ever since I became a qualified nurse."

I bet that would cost you. Remember you'd have to rent or buy the building in the first instance then fit it out with staff, patients and equipment."

"I've known people to get a building already fitted out and sometimes it is up and running – meaning it has patients and staff already in situ. I would have to make sure the books tallied before I took it on with a loan, if they didn't that would be the end of that particular home as I wouldn't want a home with debts."

"That sounds okay, but you may as well work in a nursing home as the matron or the trained nurse then you wouldn't have to worry about how much money was coming through the door to pay the bills as that would be the responsibility of the owners – mind you they could always be on your back making sure all the beds were full."

"Before I left Salisbury I used to work in the local nursing home as a health care assistant. I enjoyed the work but not the pay - it was poor. I didn't fancy becoming a registered general nurse so I left home and came to London in search of my fortune – not that I've found it. I will never forget the assistant that was found asleep in one of the bedrooms, she could find nothing wrong with having a snooze while feeding this lady her lunch. The problem with this care assistant on this particular day was that she had been out clubbing the night before and was walked home by a bloke who had insisted on staying the night but Kate didn't fancy him. Instead of showing him the door like anyone sensible she spent the night pushing him out of her bed. Another time the same assistant told one of the patient's about her love life and how she often had sex on a park bench. I can go on for ever telling you tales about what different health care assistants got up to at work and in their spare time."

"Mind you I can tell you different things that happen in our hospital between the health care assistants, nurses and doctors, most aren't squeaky clean. I have known some on nights having sex in the linen cupboard."

"Gosh, I never thought for one minute you would be telling me that, I thought all the staff in hospitals were goody goodies."

"Hilary, you must be joking, you have definitely got that wrong. If I go ahead with my dream I'll have to make sure things that happened in Salisbury don't happen in my home. Would you be interested in opening one with me, you could look after the money/office side of things?"

"I wouldn't mind, I'm sure it would be more interesting than working in Harrods but I don't have any spare cash, all my money is spent by the end of each week – I haven't any for a rainy day. I think it would be better if you got a job in a nursing home as the matron because what you'd be earning would be yours to spend as you wish and you wouldn't have to pay off a loan and I'll stay working in Harrods."

"Hilary, perhaps you're right but I'll still look into it and see what I can find. The nursing home will have to be in London as I don't want to live and work out in the sticks. Perhaps when we meet up next week I'll be working my notice at the hospital.

"Barbara, we have been sat here for a good hour, I'd better go to the counter and order two more coffees or we'll be kicked out for out staying our welcome. I'm starving. I fancy something to eat."

"Hilary, it has gone one o'clock and I'm hungry as well." said Barbara looking down at her watch.

"I'll see if I can get a couple of bread rolls." The woman behind the counter offered to fill two with cheese and ham – they were delicious. Once we finished eating and drinking we exchanged phone numbers before plodding out of the coffee bar to go our separate ways, wishing each other luck about not drinking alcohol. "If you become desperate for a drop of the hard stuff Barbara ring me, then I can try and put you off filling a glass with whatever you fancy."

"Hilary, you can do the same remember you're not on your own you have me for what it's worth." Blowing a kiss, Barbara jumped in a cab and I ran along to the tube station.

Once I got out of the tube at Covent Garden I hurried along Long Acre towards Drury Lane when I heard someone call out my name, thinking it couldn't possibly be me that this person was calling I kept walking when suddenly someone tapped me on the shoulder, turning around to see who it was I saw Bernard Small from Salisbury facing me. I hadn't seen him since I left home, Bernard was one of the many friends that joined me at the pub a few times a week for what I called a booze up – two glasses of wine.

"Bernard, what are you doing in London, have you come up for the day?"

"I was about to ask you the same question. I never dreamt I'd bump into you of all people here. I thought you were still living in Salisbury but just not visiting the pub. You used to work in that nursing home near the pub. What are you doing in London?"

"I live here and work in the accounts department of Harrods. Getting back to you why are you here?"

"I've been living and working here for the last six months the bank transferred me. I'm walking home to my bedsitter which is in Drury Lane behind the London Theatre. Where are you going?"

"Same as you, home. I live in the opposite direction, my bedsitter is across the road from the Theatre Royal."

We soon reached the T junction at Drury Lane, before parting company Bernard suggested we should meet up for a drink one evening if I wasn't dating anyone as he didn't want to step on any ones' toes.

"No, I'm not seeing anyone. I've just started going to the Wellington on the Strand, Saturday evenings where I meet up with a few friends, much like we did in Salisbury all those years ago. I'm meeting them tonight if you feel like coming along, I'll be there at about eight."

"That sounds great, I'll see you there." with that we parted company. I plodded along to my bedsitter dreaming about my old life in Salisbury and how Bernard used to make me laugh as we had the same sense of humour.

"I arrived at the Wellington just before eight, Tim was sat at the far end of the table not like last week when Wendy was sat there. As soon as Tim saw me coming towards the table he jumped to his feet and offered me the same drink as I had last Saturday. I explained I was trying to give up the booze and would like a soft drink. I also told him about Bernard and how he should be arriving in a few minutes to join in the fun. With that the side door opened and in he walked.

"Bernard, I'm over here, come and meet the gang." I called out. Tim immediately introduced himself and suggested Bernard should sit down at the table while he went and got the next round of drinks. "Bernard, what do you fancy a pint of something?"

"That sounds good to me, a pint of best bitter please." Bernard and I pulled up a couple of chairs and sat ourselves down. Wendy was quick to ask who Bernard was and how we knew each other.

"Hilary and I go back years. We bumped into each other in Long Acre this afternoon after not seeing each other for a couple of years."

"I guess you realise Hilary has become a bit of a boozer?" replied Wendy laughing out loud. I never thought for one minute that Wendy would spill the beans.

"Wendy, what you are saying can't possibly be true, I have never known Hilary to drink more than a couple of glasses of wine in an evening."

"Wendy, if I want Bernard to know about my life in London and especially my drinking habit, I'll tell him myself." Silence reigned until Tim returned with the drinks "What's the matter? I've never known you lot not to have anything to say to one another."

"I've just told Wendy to keep her mouth shut and stop gossiping about my life here in London, she was about to spill the beans to Bernard about my friend." Tim looked annoyed, "I'm going to stick up for Hilary, it's not for you to gossip about any of us Wendy. You would not like it if we said things about you which we could, quite easily. One thing we can say for sure is that you're a chatterbox and a gossip."

"I'm going." Replied Wendy getting more and more agitated and embarrassed by the minute. After getting her things together she left by the side entrance in a huff. "Tim, that was a shock to my system, I didn't expect Wendy to leave because of me telling her to shut up."

"You obviously don't know her as well as we all do. If everything is going her way, her world is wonderful but if any of us upsets her she usually leaves in a rush and goes across to the Prince of Wales in Drury Lane. We all think she must have mates that go there on a Saturday because if she hadn't she would stay here. I can guarantee she'll be back next Saturday as if nothing had gone wrong – we haven't lost her for ever."

"I hope you don't think I have a short fuse like her because I haven't. The only thing Wendy and I have in common is that we live in the same building, in fact we live next door to one another. How did you all meet her?"

"Wendy works in the sales department of the firm Robert works for."

"Which one of you is Robert?"

"Me." said Robert putting his hand up. "It's times like this when I wish I hadn't invited Wendy to join us here. Getting back to what I do, I am the production supervisor in a factory that makes car parts. The tools Tim makes in the factory he works in, our firm use."

"I'm going to introduce Hilary and Bernard to you all but before I do I'm going to tell them about myself, not that I'm very interesting. Here goes, I'm a tool maker in a factory down the road from where I live which is a high rise flat in Shepherds Bush. I live in the flat I shared with my parents but now they are no longer with me I live on my own and find it very lonely – this group has saved my life. John, who is sat next to Robert is home on leave from the R.A.F. he has come along this evening as he is an old school friend of mine and is spending his leave with me. He is very popular with the ladies as he drives a M.G. A sports car." Said Tim laughing to himself. "Mary works as a typist in the typing pool in the same factory as I work in. Now you have been introduced you can tell us a bit about yourselves."

Bernard was quick to respond. "Hilary and I used to live in Salisbury, in fact we went to the same school but were not in the same class for any subject. After leaving school a few of us arranged to meet up a couple of evenings a week in a pub – a bit like you do here. I work as a bank clerk down the road from here. I got transferred to London about six months ago. This afternoon Hilary and I bumped into each other while walking along Long Acre. Hilary suggested I came along this evening. I have a feeling coming here on a Saturday evening will suit me. Hilary, your turn."

I explained what I did as a job and where I live. I thought it best not to mention my friend Alcohol as I'm determined to give it up and before I know it I should be tea total. The evening progressed with me having soft drinks and Bernard a few pints. At around ten I decided to leave as I was determined not to be around when the group were leaving to go along to Trafalgar for the weekly dip.

"I'm going." silence reigned.

"What do you mean going?" asked Bernard looking surprised. "I'm going home, as I'm fed up with drinking soft drinks while you're all drinking alcohol and getting slowly tiddled. Before I go I must tell you that I'm not fed up with your company – just the soft drinks. Everything being equal I'll be back next Saturday - eight o'clock."

"Stay while I finish this pint then I'll walk you home. I'll only be a few minutes." Bernard soon finished his pint and we were saying our goodbyes before going out the side door on to Bow Street.

Chapter 6

"Which way shall we go, up the slope to Long Acre or through Broad Court to Drury Lane?"

"Bernard, you choose as I have a problem with going either way."

"What do you mean by a problem? You're with me so nothing untoward will happen to you this evening. Hold on to my arm, I'm going to take you up the slope to Long Acre then we can go for a coffee in the late night café. I go there quite often and the coffee is good. While in the cafe you can tell me about your problems."

"Having a coffee sounds a very good idea Bernard, as I don't want to go home. All I wanted to do was leave the pub before closing time." I went on to explain how they all go for a paddle in the fountains at Trafalgar, rain or shine after getting tiddled in the Wellington.

"I'm pleased we left when we did if that's what they do, as I'm not used to going into cold water after drinking alcohol, far too dangerous and I have had four pints of strong beer and feel a bit tiddled." Walking up the slope Bernard listened intently as I explain about the kiosks in Broad Court and how I'd befriended the rough sleepers in Long Acre last Saturday. Once we were at the top of the slope we turned right and directly in front of us were the rough sleepers that I met last weekend. Bernard seemed shocked when they came over and started chatting to me as if they were my best friends.

"Is this Graham?" asked Mary-Anne, looking Bernard up and down.

"No this is Bernard from Salisbury."

"Nice to meet you Bernard from Salisbury."

"Would you like a coffee?" called out Pete. "We have enough hot water and a couple of extra mugs – we keep them in case we have visitors." Bernard looked embarrassed. "Hilary, you can stay for a coffee but I need to go for a wee – I'm bursting." With that Bernard stepped backwards and fell on to the road hitting his head on the concrete. A black cab swerved and just missed Bernard by a couple of inches, which was a bit of luck. The driver stopped the cab, jumped out and offered to help. "As you can see I haven't a fare and you really need to be checked over at the hospital and St. Thomas's Hospital with its casualty department is only a mile and a half away. I'll take you both over and drop you off outside."

I was in shock as one minute we were talking to the rough sleepers and the next Bernard and I were getting in a cab to go to hospital. Poor Bernard didn't seem to know what was happening, I am sure he'd had more than four pints to drink. I have a feeling he had a couple before he left home – my cousin always did – for dutch courage.

Before we had time to make ourselves comfortable in the back of the cab we were getting out at the hospital and I was asking the driver how much I owed him. "Nothing it is my pleasure to be able to help you." I was very grateful as money for me is always in short supply.

Once I'd fetched the wheel chair and taken Bernard into the casualty department, explained to the receptionist what had happened, found a seat for myself and a space for Bernard and the wheel chair a health care assistant was calling out Bernard's name. I waved and she came over to wheel Bernard into a cubicle to wait and see either a trained nurse or a doctor. I remained in the main waiting area wondering what was going to happen next when I heard someone call out. "There's my friend who was kind enough to bring me here." I looked up and Bernard was pointing towards me. I couldn't believe my eyes when I saw Barbara pushing Bernard across the waiting area towards me from a cubicle.

"I didn't expect to bump into you, I only thought you worked days."

"Normally I do but they were short staffed again so I offered to work a night shift. Mind you I need the money. Any way how do you two know each other?" I explained how we'd bumped into one another in Long Acre and for old times sake we arranged to go to the pub for the evening. "Can Bernard go home, or has he got to stay in overnight?"

"As he lives alone the doctor thinks he should stay here. I'm trying to find him a bed. I'll leave him here with you while I phone around the wards. I shouldn't be too long."

Silence reigned while Bernard sat half asleep and I sat dreaming about how I was going to get back to Drury Lane and my room due to lack of money and it being far too late into the night for me to walk the mile and a half alone in London. I always remember how I walked home late at night when living with my parents in Salisbury, it was by walking along the pavement near to the edge of the road so I could be seen by car drivers and if any thing untoward happened they may have stopped to help. Barara soon returned smiling all over her face. "Bernard, I've found you a bed on Sea Ward it's on the second floor so we need to go up in the lift. Hilary, how are you getting home as there isn't a bed here for you, sorry?"

"I'm not sure, as I'm short of cash so a cab is out of the question."

"I can lend you the money but I will need it back when we meet up."

"Thanks that's kind of you Barbara. Before you take Bernard up to the ward I have some news for you regarding a nursing home you may be interested in. Bernard was reading the Evening Standard the other evening and came across an article about a nursing home that needs a matron and it is not far from here. I was going to ring you tomorrow to let you know about it."

"That's good news Hilary. I'll be going home to bed as soon as I finish this shift but I will be getting up again around two. I'll be looking forward to your call during the afternoon."

"I'll ring about three."

"If you hang on here while I take Bernard up to the ward I'll come back with a few bob so you can get a cab."

"Please don't take too long as I don't fancy getting into a black cab on my own after midnight, especially on a Saturday/Sunday – it's already quarter to twelve.

Barbara where do you call home? I have your phone number but not your address."

"When you ring me I'll tell you, it's not far from here and I doubt if it's far from your place, where ever that is."

"My place is in Drury Lane across the road from the back of the Theatre Royal."

"Gosh, that's a shock, I had no idea where you lived but I never dreamt in my wildest dreams it would be there. The rent alone must cost you an arm and a leg for a little room, your wages must be very good. When you stayed in hospital for that one night I didn't get the chance to look at your notes as I didn't come on duty till eight in the morning and you were going home before I blinked and your notes were taken away by the admin staff so this is a real shock to my system."

"When you decide to tell me where you live, most probably I'll be in shock."

"No you won't. I live in a two bedroom flat. The entrance is next door to a paper shop over the other side of the river. I have lived there for years, it was part of my divorce settlement in fact I'm laughing all over my face as my ex pays the rent and has to continue paying it unless I find myself another husband and I won't find one of them – I'm not daft. I won't let any man move in with me for keeps. I have arrangements with men that I go out with and that is that they can stay for the odd night or weekend, come for a pretend holiday but for no longer than a week. See you in a minute." Smiling to herself Barbara left pushing Bernard as fast as she dare to the lift.

It seemed ages before she returned with a five pound note. "Hilary, you must remember this is a loan, I need it back when we next meet up. Bernard said to let you know that he will ring you during the week to arrange about going to the Wellington next Saturday evening."

"That's good. I thought he would be walking out of my life for ever after making a fool of himself this evening. I'm pleased he is not embarrassed about what happened. I don't think he liked having to speak to the rough sleepers and to think they knew my name seemed to be the last straw for him."

"He didn't mention them to me."

"As soon as they said hi he decided he needed the loo and before turning around to go down the hill to the loo he fell over backwards on to the road, the rest is history."

"I can't stand here talking, I have work to do. I'm looking forward to you ringing tomorrow to give me the low down on this nursing home. Do you have the address for it?"

"Yeah, it is down a street towards the South bank from the Strand. I have a feeling the home is called Vill and the street is Villier Street. Barbara before I go on my way will there be black cabs waiting in the car park or will I have to pick one up in the street?"

"There should be a few waiting outside the main door."

"Good, cheers."

With that we parted company me over to the window to have a look for a cab and Barbara back to her patients. Luckily for me a black cab was just pulling up. I rushed out the door to the car park. "Hop in love." Said the driver, after I explained where I wanted to go.

Within minutes I was getting out and running across the road to my bedsitter. I was so pleased to be home and couldn't wait to get into bed.

Chapter 7

I didn't have a very good night's sleep, I laid awake for most of it. If I wasn't worrying about Bernard and how he banged his head I was thinking of Barbara and the nursing home and how she may become a matron and me becoming the accountant.

Eventually sleep came and I didn't wake until half ten. After eating breakfast I rang the hospital to enquire about Bernard, he seemed okay and was waiting for the doctor to do his round, fingers crossed he will be going home later today.

As the sun was shining and having a couple of hours to spare I went for a walk across to the Covent Garden Craft Market where I sat in the café and over a cup of coffee had a chat with Stella, who is one of the stall holders. She was very pleased to see the sun as this meant there should be plenty of punters, in fact she was on a high as she had already made twenty five pounds by selling animal pens this morning. "If I go on selling pens like this, I may be able to book a holiday."

"Where are you thinking of going?" I asked looking excited for her. "I would love to go to Spain, Cost de Sol. Selling pens at a pound a piece won't get me far so I will be spending my holiday in England. Where ever I go it must be out in the sticks, as I need a break from city life for a couple of weeks. Please don't get me wrong, I love London Town and wouldn't live anywhere else permanently. A holiday in the middle of a field would be good as long as there were no cows in the field."

"Stella, cows don't hurt anyone, they just make long deep sound called a moo. I know someone who stayed in a tent in a field and nearly jumped out of their skin when the cow mooed in the entrance to the tent. Who are you thinking of going on this holiday with?"

"A mate, she is richer and posher than me. I doubt if she will want to go camping but I will try and persuade her. The thing is she lives in an apartment behind Selfridges in Oxford Street and I have a room above a shop over in Camdem Town. We have never been to each others places as we're both embarrassed about where each other lives. I'm embarrassed by her posh place and she's upset about my dump. We've known each other for years in fact we went to school together until one morning she came into the class room and before the teacher arrived, stood at the front of the class and announced that her parents were sending her to a private girls' school in Brighton and she would be leaving on Friday to board at Roedean School. We were all in shock as we enjoyed her company and we had no idea that she may be leaving let alone knowing her parents were rich enough to send her to a boarding school. I didn't meet up with her again for quite a few years. It was all very strange, I was stood dreaming on the platform at Oxford Circus Tube Station when this person tapped me on the shoulder and said hi - it was Cynthia. We have kept in touch ever since, once a week we go to the Wellington for a Gin and sometimes go on to the Savoy Hotel. When we meet up next Tuesday I'll ask her about going on holiday together. Most probably I'll have to keep the peace by going to stay in some posh hotel in Berkshire, which I have done before."

"Stella, she sounds a real snob. If camping isn't good enough for her why not suggest going on the Norfolk Broads in a fancy boat. If neither of these ideas suit her find someone else to go with. I'm sure you must know someone who isn't as fussy and needs a holiday."

"I do, but Cynthia is good company and enjoys a few drinks. She's not like some people I know that only drink tea or coffee." My face must have been a picture as silence reigned. All I could do was sit and think about my drinking habit and how Barbara and I are trying to get off the booze and Stella wants to go on holiday with a friend that drinks.

"I must go in a moment to make a very important phone call that may change my life. Before I go I have something to say, I used to drink heavily and have

finished up having to visit Alcoholics Anonymous once a week. If I were in your shoes I'd try to give up the booze before it takes over your life and you finish up going to A.A. for the rest of your days. Remember once an alcoholic always an alcoholic." Stella looked shocked "After telling you that I'm going, I may see you here next Sunday at the same time. Cheerio Stella."

By the time I'd walked around the stalls and had a chat with other stall holders it was time for me to hurry home to make my call to Barbara.

After about five minutes Barbara answered my call. "Hi Hilary, I've only just woken up, I was exhausted after a very busy night. I'm looking forward to hearing about this nursing home."

"Bernard read in the Evening Standard how the matron had left this home in a rush. The only reason he mentioned it to me was because it's near Trafalgar Square and he thought I may have heard about it, but I hadn't. The matron left because she stole £500 out of the medicine cupboard, the money was put in there for safe keeping as it was the weekend and the trained nurse on duty hadn't the key to the safe. On the Monday morning the owners went to get the money out of the medicine cupboard and the money was missing so they called the police." The matron admitted taking the cash so was sacked without notice. In one breath I feel sorry for the matron as she is hardly likely to get another job but then again, she shouldn't have taken the money so it serves her right. The strange thing is the man that looked after the finances walked out at the same time."

"I bet he knew about her taking the money, perhaps they planned it together. I wonder if they were having an affair and needed the cash to go away for a dirty weekend."

"I hadn't given that a thought. If we manage to get jobs at this home we may hear what actually happened, as no doubt the staff will be gossiping about it. Barbara, what are we going to do? Are we going to walk to this home at some point and take a look at the outside and if we like what we see, ring the bell?"

"That sounds a good idea. I better give you my address and explain how to get here so you can call around. Walk along the Strand towards Trafalgar Square from the Wellington Pub – stay on the right hand side.

Eventually you will come across a sign that says Bedford Street turn into this street. My flat is on the left hand side, number 124, you can't miss it as the front door is the first door past the paper shop. Ring the bell then I'll come down and let you in. Call around about six, between now and then I'll have had time to cook us a meal. After eating and chewing the cud we can walk over to this nursing home as I don't think its far from here, unless you have something else planned for this evening?"

"No, nothing planned. Thanks for the invite, I'll see you at 124 Bedford Street at six o'clock."

Chapter 8

It wasn't long before I was ringing the bell at number 124. After a good five minutes the door opened and their stood Barbara all glammed up in a cocktail dress as if she was going to a posh do.

"You look posh. Have I come around the wrong evening, are you going somewhere special?"

"No Hilary, you have the right evening, I love dressing up especially when I'm expecting a visitor, even if they're only coming round for a coffee I put on a creation that I have managed to find cheap in a charity shop. Please don't feel embarrassed it's just one of the things I enjoy doing. Anyway, come in and follow me upstairs." Up we plodded to a very upmarket apartment. Looking around I felt slightly uncomfortable as the apartment seemed the sort of place where someone would be coming out of the kitchen at any moment having cooked the supper to announce 'supper is ready' but thank goodness this didn't happen - we waited on ourselves. We ate cottage pie followed by ice cream, it was yummy.

We chatted non stop about different things for a good half an hour, alcohol was not on the agenda in fact the word alcohol was not mentioned - thank God. I didn't even see any empty bottles. It was as if Barbara had never drunk alcohol at work or anywhere else.

The A to Z was the next thing on our minds, as we needed to look up Villier Street. It didn't take us long to find it on the map once Barbara had found the magnifying glass to use, as the map was so small and the writing even smaller.

"It's only a few minutes walk from here, we need to go to the Strand, cross the road then walk towards Trafalgar and we should see the sign for Villier Street on the left hand side. The nursing home is about half way along Villier Street on the left in fact it is opposite the entrance to the Embankment Gardens. Hilary we need to make a decision, shall we go and look at the outside of the nursing home this evening or leave it until tomorrow as I've a day off? I don't go back to work until Tuesday afternoon."

"I have a couple of days holiday due to me so I could take tomorrow off. I can ring Harrods in the morning saying my parents are ill and I need to go home or I could say I'm in Salisbury as mum's sick either way I can meet up with you tomorrow."

"Hilary, I think because Villier Street is so close to here and it's still day light we should go and take a peep at the street this evening. If we like what we can see of the nursing home you can arrange to take the day off, then we can go back tomorrow to take a closer look at the outside and if we like the look of it, we can ring the bell. Fingers crossed we may be giving in our notices by the end of the week."

It wasn't long before we were walking down Villier Street. "Hilary, I like what I can see, the street itself is quite up market which means the nursing home should be the same. What do you think?"

"Same as you. I look forward to taking a closer look at the outside and of course the inside tomorrow. Barbara, if we aren't going to the nursing home this evening shall we go into that wine bar for a glass of vino it looks interesting?" I said nodding my head towards the entrance.

"I was wondering how long it would be before one of us mentioned booze. I hope you noticed I didn't have any wine on show in my flat and also I didn't offer you any." laughed Barbara.

"I bet you had some hidden in a cupboard."

"That is for me to know and you to find out." We wandered into the bar with the intension of only having the one glass of wine but finished up having three each which equated to having one bottle of wine between us. Once we had drunk the wine we were on a high to drink more but the price stopped us. Drinking the wine was not good news as we had to walk home feeling squiffy and knew that we wouldn't be fit to visit the nursing home in the morning. "Hilary, I think you ought to stay at my place tonight, the bed is made up in the spare room."

"Thanks that sounds a good idea."

Once back at the apartment Barbara opened one of the cupboards and there in front of us was the wine store. "Here's my wine. As we only had three small glasses in the wine bar do you fancy another glass or two?" I thought for a minute before replying "Okay but just the one."

"Hilary, you can choose which bottle I open Red, White or Rosa as you're my guest.

"We were drinking Red in the bar so we better continue drinking Red please." With that Barbara found two wine glasses in another cupboard. "I thought you may have got rid of your wine glasses like I suggested and we would be drinking out of coffee mugs."

"You must be joking. I hardly ever do what people suggest I should. I make my own mind up and I decided to keep these glasses as I thought one day they may come in useful and they have. Cheers Hilary." One glass led to another until we finished the bottle. How I got into bed I don't know, but I did, thank God. I woke up with a thick head and found myself still in the clothes I wore out to Villiers Street. I managed to get out of bed and wander out on to the landing where I thought I would see Barbara's door open as she would be up and about, instead I found her door closed with a note sellotaped to it for me to read. The note explained that she would not be getting up until at least midday due to a hangover and if I needed Alka Salza they're on the kitchen table with a glass ready for me to use, also I could feel free to use the phone to ring Harrods – so I did.

After making the phone call I walked back to my bed sitter for a wash and change of clothes. This didn't take as long as I expected so I rang Barbara before returning to her apartment to make sure she's up and raring to go over to Villiers Street and the nursing home. She was quick to answer the phone and suggested I should arrive at her apartment around two. "By the time we have walked over to Vills the patients may be having there afternoon snooze so the trained nurse should have time for a chat and show us around once we explain that I'm interested in the matron's job and you in the office job. What do you think Hilary?"

"That sounds good to me."

"I'll be waiting for you out on the pavement. Before I hang up I must ask how you're feeling after drinking all that wine?"

"My head was spinning this morning, thanks for leaving out the Alka Salza, I needed them and they worked a treat, thank God. How is your head?"

"When I got out of bed my head was like I imagined a really bad migraine would be like. I could hardly open my eyes let alone move my head, I'm okay now, thank goodness. If I am offered the job as matron and I take it I am promising myself that I will not be socialising in the wine bar across from the nursing home. The wine was very nice thank you very much but far to expensive for me, it cost an arm and a leg."

"Barbara I loved it in there, the music was fantastic – what I can remember of it and the wine well that will take some beating. I shall be visiting again, even if I don't get the job, I shall make the effort to go back for a glass of vino on a pay day."

"I'm going now, we can continue this conversation when we meet up in half an hour." Bang went the receiver.

Barbara was waiting as promised but looking completely different from last night. This afternoon she looks like she could be a nurse as she has hardly any make up on and her hair has been tied up in a bun instead of having it flowing down her back, she'd also changed the type of clothes she was wearing to drab slacks with a plain long sleeved top – very nice, but very different from last night's bright and breezy look.

"You look bright and breezy this afternoon, and I look as dull as dish water, complete opposite to last night." Called out Barbara when she saw me walking towards her.

"I put this on because of how you looked last night. I found this little number in the back of a cupboard. I didn't want to be known as your dull friend."

"Very nice it is too."

Silence reigned as we walked over to Villier Street – alone with our thoughts. Barbara trying to get her head clear before speaking to the Staff Nurse in charge this afternoon and me wondering what is going to happen when we knock on the door.

We soon arrived at the entrance to the Embankment Gardens where we stood back against the gate to take a long hard look at the outside of the nursing home. Windows were clean, curtains hung straight, the brass on the door was extra clean – it seemed like royalty could be arriving.

"Hilary, it looks good to me, lets go and ring the bell." We gave each other a hug and wished each other luck before crossing the road to the front door. Barbara rang the door bell. It took a good ten minutes before a health care assistant answered and invited us in to sit and wait for the trained nurse.

"Fingers crossed Hilary, this could be the start of our new career."

The End

Printed in Great Britain
by Amazon